The Gingerbread Man

by Jackie Walter and Marcus Cutler

W

FRANKLIN WATTS

LONDON•SYDNEY

Long ago, there lived a little old woman
and a little old man in a little old house.
One day, the old woman made
a little man out of gingerbread.

She gave him currants for his eyes.

She gave him a cherry for his mouth.

Then she put him in the oven to bake.

The old woman and the old man
were hungry. They couldn't wait to eat
the gingerbread man.
Soon, the gingerbread man was cooked.
The old woman took the tray
out of the oven.

The gingerbread man jumped up
from the tray and ran away!

The gingerbread man hopped

out of the window.

"Don't eat me!" he shouted.

"Stop, stop!" cried the little old woman

and the little old man.

But the gingerbread man did not look back. He ran down the lane, shouting, "Run, run, as fast as you can! You can't catch me, I'm the gingerbread man!"

Soon, the gingerbread man met a pig.

"Stop!" said the pig. "I want to eat you."

But the gingerbread man was too fast.

He ran on, shouting,

"Run, run, as fast as you can!

You can't catch me,

I'm the gingerbread man!"

Soon, the gingerbread man met a cow.

"Stop!" said the cow. "I want to eat you."

But the gingerbread man ran faster,

shouting,

"Run, run, as fast as you can!

You can't catch me,

I'm the gingerbread man!"

Next, the gingerbread man met a horse.

"Stop!" said the horse.

"I want to eat you."

But the gingerbread man ran
even faster, shouting,
"Run, run, as fast as you can!
You can't catch me,
I'm the gingerbread man!"

Then the gingerbread man came to
a river.

"Oh no!" he cried. "I cannot swim.
They will catch me!"

A sly fox saw the gingerbread man.
He licked his lips. "I can eat him
for my dinner," the fox said to himself.

"I can help you cross the river,"
said the fox. "Jump on my tail,
and I will swim across."
"No, you will eat me,"
said the gingerbread man.
"I will not," said the fox.

So the gingerbread man climbed onto
the fox's tail. They started to cross
the river.

Soon the fox said, "You are too heavy for my tail. Climb onto my back." And the gingerbread man did.

Next the fox said, "You are too heavy for my back. Climb onto my head." And the gingerbread man did.

When they got to the other side
of the river, the fox tossed his head.

The gingerbread man flew up,
high into the air, then SNAP!
And that was the end
of the gingerbread man.

Story order

Look at these 5 pictures and captions.
Put the pictures in the right order
to retell the story.

1

The fox tossed up his head.

2

The gingerbread man climbed onto
the fox's tail.

3

The gingerbread man ran from the pig.

4

The gingerbread man jumped off the tray.

5

The gingerbread man came to a river.

Guide for Independent Reading

This series is designed to provide an opportunity for your child to read on their own. These notes are written for you to help your child choose a book and to read it independently.

In school, your child's teacher will often be using reading books which have been banded to support the process of learning to read. Use the book band colour your child is reading in school to help you make a good choice. *The Gingerbread Man* is a good choice for children reading at Turquoise Band in their classroom to read independently. The aim of independent reading is to read this book with ease, so that your child enjoys the story and relates it to their own experiences.

About the book

A little old woman bakes a gingerbread man. But this little man does NOT want to be eaten, and he runs away as fast as he can!

Before reading

Help your child to learn how to make good choices by asking:
"Why did you choose this book? Why do you think you will enjoy it?"
Look at the cover together and ask: "What do you think the story will be about?" Ask your child to think of what they already know about the story context. Then ask your child to read the title aloud.
Ask: "What do you think the gingerbread man is doing in the story?" Remind your child that they can sound out a word in syllable chunks if they get stuck.
Decide together whether your child will read the story independently or read it aloud to you.

During reading

Remind your child of what they know and what they can do independently. If reading aloud, support your child if they hesitate or ask for help by telling the word. If reading to themselves, remind your child that they can come and ask for your help if stuck.

After reading

Support comprehension by asking your child to tell you about the story. Use the story order puzzle to encourage your child to retell the story in the right sequence, in their own words. The correct sequence can be found on the next page.

Help your child think about the messages in the book that go beyond the story and ask: "Why do you think the fox is able to trick the gingerbread man at the end?" Give your child a chance to respond to the story: "Did you have a favourite part? What would you do if your favourite biscuit ran away?"

Extending learning

Help your child understand the story structure by using the same sentence patterning and adding different elements. "Let's make up a new story about the gingerbread man. Who might he meet this time and how could he escape? What might he do differently?"

In the classroom, your child's teacher may be teaching use of punctuation marks. Ask your child to identify some question marks and exclamation marks in the story and then ask them to practise reading each of the whole sentences with appropriate expression.

Franklin Watts
First published in Great Britain in 2021
by The Watts Publishing Group

Copyright © The Watts Publishing Group 2021

Series Editors: Jackie Hamley and Melanie Palmer
Series Advisors: Dr Sue Bodman and Glen Franklin
Series Designers: Peter Scoulding and Cathryn Gilbert

A CIP catalogue record for this book is
available from the British Library.

ISBN 978 1 4451 7702 1 (hbk)
ISBN 978 1 4451 7704 5 (pbk)
ISBN 978 1 4451 7703 8 (library ebook)
ISBN 978 1 4451 8150 9 (ebook)

Printed in China

Franklin Watts
An imprint of
Hachette Children's Group
Part of The Watts Publishing Group
Carmelite House
50 Victoria Embankment
London EC4Y 0DZ

An Hachette UK Company
www.hachette.co.uk

www.franklinwatts.co.uk

Answer to Story order: 4, 3, 5, 2, 1